Praise for The Sound of Starfall

"This is the best novella I've ever read."
— **Bibliotheory**

.

"This was a beautifully written novella!"
- **Bookish Coffee**

.

"There aren't many books I can recall that have made me feel true fear in the way that The Sound of Starfall does."
— **Joshua Walker, author of *The Song of the Sleepers***

.

"Scott is truly a dark fantasy master."
- **Kristen Shafer, SFF Insiders**

BY SCOTT PALMER

The Sound of Starfall

A Memory of Song

THE SOUND OF STARFALL

A Prelude to the Last Ballad

SCOTT PALMER

THE NYTEWOOD PRESS

To...

anyone who was told they couldn't do it but went and did it anyway.

CONTENTS

AUTHOR'S NOTE

This whole story started with a map. The world of The Remembered Lands was, in my mind, always going to be far bigger than just one story. I want to show you the history behind everything, the cultures that make that history rich, and I want to show you glimpses of big characters that you may not have gotten in the main series. This novella serves as a companion to The Last Ballad, and subsequent novellas will continue to reveal more of the rich history of The Remembered Lands that was lost to time.

The story picks up about 3000 years before the start of A Memory Of Song, just hours before the sky fell. I sincerely hope you enjoy *The Sound of Starfall*.

Until the next one,

Scott Palmer

Every act of creation is first an act of destruction.

Pablo Picasso

THE WARLOCK

Five Hours to Starfall

THE SKY WAS BLEEDING when Adeqor woke. His eyes were stuck on the falling star that cut it apart.

"It's getting bigger every hour." The words were gravel in his mouth.

Adeqor lay on his silken sheets drenched in salty sweat. The dream eaters had been making the nightmares more vivid now that they were so close, and he had suffered much through the night with little sleep. He sat up and took a deep breath. The soothsayers had predicted the end three days ago, and Adeqor knew they were never wrong about much else. It couldn't be much longer until it was over. Hours maybe. Appreciating every moment up above would be necessary to avoid the regret of it in the tunnels below. He only sat for a few moments before getting up to find Sera.

If Sera really wants to go through this, I'll do it.

The apartments opened up from the bedchamber like a vast sea of precious stone and metal glinting below crystal skies. Golden blades of dawn pierced through the glass dome ceiling and brought the brilliant white and black-veined marble floors to life with its light. Deep red rugs made of thick Gwelari satin lined the floors in stark contrast to the shining marble tile. Tapestries and artwork by the finest artists in all the Remembered Lands adorned the walls at every turn, framed with glistening platinum. They were lit from under by flames flickering in sconces of pure gold. Tables of red cedar and black walnut stretched out from all corners of the main room, topped with horns of plenty and candles of beeswax and scented oils. Incense from Neira and far off Arish Pura burned all day and night, keeping the apartment clean from lingering sicknesses with their infused magics. It was a complete shame for such luxuries to be lost. *But the star will burn it all. You've seen it in your dreams.*

The hearth crackled a hot glow as Sera sat cross-legged beside it, tinkering with the many small pots before her. They were filled with substances of various smell and viscosity that Sera used to craft potions with her beauty magics.

"Have you thought more about it yet?" Adeqor chewed his finger nail.

Sera stopped, a shaking hand hovering above the red gold mortar Bazal had gifted them on their wedding night so many years ago. *Everyone had shown up for us, all with gifts to impress... They thought*

Insa and I would save them... She peered at Adeqor through the cloud of brown smoke floating up from her mortar, the bags beneath her blue eyes red and puffy from tears.

"I've thought about it." Her expression was blank. Adeqor had never been good at reading her, but it didn't take much to see that something inside of her was completely broken. She had gone back and forth between wanting to go below or staying up above to watch the sky fall on them. Both were deaths of a different kind.

"Have you decided?" he said. Sera's lower lip quivered. She nodded.

"I want to go down. Yora and Ren are going," she said, and her tears fell as she leaned in to Adeqor for comfort. "They decided they'd go this morning. Yora only just told me." Adeqor wrapped his arms around her and held her close to him. He bathed in her warmth, and her perfume of dragonlily soothed his shame as he kissed her neck.

Only the best for you, Sera. Whatever it takes to make up for all I've put you through.

"Then we'll go down." Adeqor's stomach twisted into knots at the thought of it actually happening. They would need to use Insa's old spells if they were to go down to the tunnels, and those dark magics came with dark consequences. Even just a taste of those spells had taken bites out of Adeqor's soul and blocked his heart from feeling. "Nine!" Adeqor called out.

Adeqor's servant, Nine, came in through a large white oak door, wearing an off-white toga stained with oils, tinctures, and what Adeqor thought looked like blood.

"Master?" Nine asked. He stood as straight and strong as a statue.

"Is that blood on you?" Adeqor studied him. *This filth...* Nine looked down.

"Just from the scullery, master. They're butchering everything down there for the last feast."

"Hmph." Adeqor had long hated the confidence of this domestic fool. Nine acted like Adeqor's previous eight servants were lesser than he. *And they were, weren't they? Not all blood is velvet red, no, some is stained with gold and purple. It is your mother who was the fool for allowing a domestic to come forth inside her.* Adeqor cracked his neck side to side and dismissed the whole thing. He didn't have time to pick at old scabs. "We're going to need to eat. And get us Soma. We're going to have a long day, and to face it sober would be madness."

"Master." Nine confirmed with a stiff nod and hurried off.

"When are you going to ask him?" Sera said. Adeqor puffed his cheeks. Nine was the living reminder of one of Adeqor's biggest shames. "He's your brother, Adee. Or have you forgotten that, too?"

Adeqor's chest tightened. *Half brother...* "Today. Before we go, I will ask him." Adeqor hoped he was lying.

Sera went back to her potions. She used to work her magics in their private amphitheatre, but now her tinkering had spilled out onto the tables and floor. Adeqor knew it was her comfort, so he said nothing as he stepped over the various bottles and trays and walked out to the balcony terrace alone.

Above, the sky howled like some demon descending. A piercing, echoing thunder that stormed on and on. The sound of Starfall swallowed every thought. He walked to the edge, the marble railing cool on his fingers, and took another deep breath. Outside of the magnificent city walls, the black mass of Abori warriors and dream eaters were setting up camp. An army so vast they seemed to melt out of the northern sky.

No army had ever breached the shining gold walls of Ailar. The Great Golden City was the sanctuary of the Yehvenki Warlocks. And the Warlocks ruled the world. But Adeqor, and every other Warlock for the last century, knew how it would end whenever the Abori warriors came for them. *This... was different. Personal.*

This was the end.

Every night, the Abori dream eaters provided the race of Warlocks with visions of their own deaths. In nightmares, the Abori breach the golden walls of Ailar, acid dripping from their ears from the Kiss of Silence, burning their city to ash and butchering their children. Every person who walked in Yehven understood that when the Abori came, the Words of power would cease to work, and folks would soon be begging for death. To be bound up by the Abori and forced to watch the sky rip apart was the worst kind of death.

The Abori sang magics of the Earth and Nature, and not at all the eldritch darkness that flowed inside of Adeqor and his kin. The Abori were a thunderstorm and Ailar was but a golden thunder rod. This was the end. A literal living nightmare. They'd known it for a century. But it wasn't easy to accept. And Adeqor knew one person who may know something he didn't. There was one shred of hope clinging to the underbelly of the golden city. One vein of shining gold still left to mine.

If you don't go ask him, you will never live with yourself down below.

Adeqor gripped the railing again, his tawny knuckles stark against the veined white marble. He hadn't left his tower complex in decades. His black beard had grown long and sharp, and his hair was down past his own arse now. *They won't even know you anymore.* The thought of leaving filled his head with an aching fog. He wasn't even sure if anyone would recognize him after so long in recluse.

You will forever regret it if you don't ask him.

He walked back into his chambers and pulled his purple cloak, the colour of masters, tight against his frail body.

"I have to go see Insa," Adeqor barely choked the words out.

"*Now?*" Sera halted her tinkering and rushed up. "Of all times? I thought you were done with Insa."

"I need to know if he finished our work. I need to know if he met *them.*"

"You're not going to leave me in this alone, are you?"

Her voice cracked, but Adeqor didn't reply.

"If Insa found a god forsaken way out of this, don't leave me to this alone. Please, Adee." Sera sobbed, tears rolling down her cheeks.

Adeqor was unsure if she was crying because of him or because of everything else. It brought him back to the days when he was still composing his symphonies of madness with Insa. Every day, she'd worried about losing him to the Words. He put his hand on her back, but Adeqor knew that not even his touch could ease the fear of what was before them.

"I won't leave you. I will be back, Sera. I just need to ask him," Adeqor said. Sera nodded wordlessly and turned back to her potions. Her face was void of anything that resembled joy. Adeqor looked at the glass tubes and bottles in front of her, the scattered utensils on trays blotted with various substances. The red gold mortar that Adeqor was so proud of was cast aside, with black stains on the side from whatever had boiled over inside of it. *This wasn't her comfort, it's the only distraction she has from* you. *She hates you now. She hates what you are.*

Nine had returned with a breakfast of poached quail eggs on a fresh half loaf with honey-glazed tomatoes all drizzled in a golden cream of pearl sauce.

And it tasted like piss. Adeqor hadn't enjoyed food the same since the star appeared in the sky, but he ate it anyway, stubbornly, as it could be one of his last real meals. *The Ailaryan Order will probably have magics to null hunger down there. In the New World, food will be a mere memory.*

Two drops of Soma in their citrus wine and Adeqor was pleasantly floating towards the immense arched doorway to leave. He hesitated, tracing the Words of holding that he'd carved with his own hands into the smooth white oak door. Pillars of purple marble arched fifty feet above his head, carved with the likenesses of Sorcerer Queens, bat-winged imps, and exotic gods. The Sorcerers had built these doors to keep anything out. *Or in...* Adeqor had never meant to leave this room again. *No one will ever know the hero you are for locking yourself away. No one will ever know what you might have saved them from...* It had been twenty-seven years since he had stepped through that door. Twenty-seven years since the Words nearly ate his soul and turned him darker than demons. *You might never come back if you leave now. You know that. Finding Insa might be the last thing you ever do. Only Karaat knows what he's become after all these years...*

Adeqor felt like some kind of undead wraith stepping back into its living body, ready to alight the world below. He was hovering in the ruddy warm glow that was his new life, afraid to re-enter the darkness that shrouded his old. Adeqor pushed the heavy doors open. Still, a strange fear clung to him. A crippling anxiety that forbade him to move. He hadn't left his apartment in so long because his work had been too much for him. The indulgence of his colleagues sickened him. The guilt had crippled him. So he had stepped away from it. *Hid* away from it in his tower of luxury. But now the thought of *what could have been* consumed him. He had to know if Insa had finished their work. He *had* to know. So he forced one foot to move, then the other. With a Word, he called the spirits of fire to bring hundreds of unlit sconces to life. In their blushing light, he traipsed down the staircase that lived in the bowels of the glass domed tower.

Not half way down the stairwell, the sight of a body soaking in a pool of blood seized Adeqor's legs. The dead man's purple cloak was torn to shreds from what looked like dozens of stab wounds. He had been mauled, sloppily and desperately.

Adeqor knelt down and turned the corpse over. He held a hand to his mouth. Fear soured his stomach. It was Dante. *But who would kill a master?* Adeqor shivered. Every part of him wanted to turn back to his tower. *You should have never come out. It's been too long...* but he shook those thoughts away and carried on slowly until he reached the entrance hall of the tower at ground level.

The Golden Guards slept and lived in the chamber directly below, protecting the entrance hall. There should have been dozens of them, but Adeqor saw only one. The guard saw him coming and sprinted towards him with a sword in hand. *He should have bowed when he saw you.*

"Drop your weapon, guard. Don't you see this cloak?" Adeqor called out. The guard's eye twitched, and he gripped his sword tighter. He wasn't even wearing a helmet. Golden Guards were required to be fully armoured. "Haruka!" Adeqor sang.

The guard smirked; he twirled his sword in his fingertips—remarkably adept, just as the Warlocks had trained them to be. Adeqor's heart dropped in his chest. The Word of obedience should bring a person to their knees.

Then he noticed the swollen scars where the guard's ears should be. *Acid in the ears... The Kiss of Silence...* A terrible fear rushed through Adeqor at the thought of his magics not working. He'd seen this in his nightmares. The Kiss of Silence was what the Abori used to deafen themselves to the Warlocks' magics. *The guards have gone mad...*

The guard rushed him. With a Word, Adeqor called the spirits of Earth and opened a hole below the guard's feet. The guard disappeared into it, and the stone closed up smoothly.

Adeqor knelt down to catch his breath. What would bring this guard to attack him? *What would make him think he even stood a chance? Why did he deafen himself with acid? Turn back. To Sera. Turn back...* But to his surprise, he carried on. If he was capable of loving in the way he used to, he may have turned back to Sera. But he could only care about himself now. About his life's work. He had lost his soul to hubris years ago, in Insa's laboratory. The Words had eaten all of the good parts of his heart and left him wanting. *Always wanting... Insa, old friend, I pray you've got good news for me.*

The outside world was so close he could smell it. The rank odour of the city brought with it sour memories. The prospect of stepping into the streets of Ailar again made him sick. *And now, of all times, now...* He walked barefoot along the crimson silk rugs of Ni'An, towards the massive doors of black opal. Statues of green garnet carved into various likenesses of Karaat snaked up the walls and hung from the ceiling like crystal bats. With a Word, the monolithic doors swung open. And before he could take a step outside, Adeqor heard heavy footsteps behind him. More guards appeared. *Fuck. Two this time. They think you're old and tired. That you lost your edge locked away in that tower. They're not afraid.*

Adeqor felt a breeze on his back coming in from outside and smiled. He whispered a Word, and the wind carried it to the first guard, who hadn't been Kissed, and burst his eardrums. He fell over with blood pouring out of his nose and eyes. The second one was unphased and came for him. With a Word, Adeqor called the spirits of Fire to eat the heat from the guard's blood. The guard fell over in an instant, cold and dead. This close, Adeqor noticed his ears were red and swollen from the Kiss. *What is happening here? Some kind of rebellion?* Adeqor shook his head.

When Adeqor stepped foot upon the gold-paved streets outside, a sound like droning thunder consumed him. It erased the things he remembered about the outside world—the unwieldy cattle wayns bulking with produce, the shifty merchants shouting wares, the sullen clanking of chains, and the droning of the pyramid singers as they wove their symphonies in the clouds. Nothing was as it used to be. The star was tearing the sky apart, and the ripping sound of it ate all else. Adeqor's memories of a shining gold city were replaced with the smell of sulphur seeping out of the sky.

The morning was warm and damp, and the gold brick was slick with dew cooling the bottoms of Adeqor's feet. *You hid away in your tower and the world went on without you...* Adeqor stopped at the base of one of the grand pyramids of Ailar, the tip stretched all the way up into the pink clouds of dawn. The Sorcerers constructed the pyramids with solid blocks of blue diamond and carved the gems with Words of grandeur. There was a time when Adeqor couldn't understand why the Sorcerers had veiled the world with their magics, why they felt the need to make beautiful things even more beautiful. It wasn't until the Words bit into Adeqor's soul that he truly understood that the Sorcerers had no choice—the Words of Karaat had eaten them and left them helpless inside of their own bodies.

The pink sun lit the pyramids like lanterns, and the surface shimmered like an ocean of stone. Oily black stones that were said to be hearts of fallen stars holding alien magics, incomprehensible even to Insa, crowned the pyramids.

The pyramids were massive echo chambers where Warlocks known as Singers projected their Words of power into the clouds. Once the clouds became fat with magics, the Words fell down upon entire populations like rain, leaving folks at the will of the masters. Nine had told him that since the soothsayers had predicted the end, the Singers had left their posts. The Words had stopped falling, and the people fought back. Adeqor had told Sera that there was no way it could be true. *Now you see it with your own eyes, and still, don't want to believe it...*

The tower streets of the aristocrats were more calm. Most of the residents had either gone to the tunnels already or were hiding safely away in their palaces. Down in the lower city, though, where Insa did his work so as not to be detected by snooping masters, it was anarchy. Ellorin and her Banshees howled screams of death as they murdered any who uttered an unauthorized Word. It was the Banshees that protected the world from the Words spreading out of control. And their method was extermination.

Adeqor walked through the streets and felt as if he had awoken into his nightmares. He stepped over bodies, both Human and animal strewed out across the streets in pieces. He staggered past troughs of stagnant sewage steaming under the hot sun and inky blotches of dried blood baked onto the gold bricks. Shattered glass and shards of pottery crunched beneath each step beneath and left not a mark on his bare feet. The slaves and smallfolk had gone mad with a dark fever, performing sacrifices and sex orgies in the open streets.

"The comet will save us." A bald woman stood atop a barrel wearing nothing but a blanket over her shoulders. "Karaat has told me true."

"The prophet has spoken," a small crowd of pallid citizens recited in unison. "The comet will save us."

A man clutched Adeqor by the arm and flashed toothless gums as he choked out incoherent words that smelled like stale cider. Adeqor shook him off and felt a chill roll down his spine as the would-be prophet grinned at him and chomped her teeth.

Priests of Karaat burned effigies of Him on pyres. Enslaved covered in scars and tattoos, still wearing broken chains around their wrists, staggered drunk in the streets. *They will be busy on this eve.* Adeqor shuddered at the thought of small folk speaking Words of power.

The city had fallen apart. Adeqor knew this day would come. Even so, it made him sick to witness it.

We went too far, Insa. Too far. We are not the Creators... Pray you at least contacted Them. Pray our work was worth it...

The indulgence of his country folk had driven Adeqor into his own little exile. He thought he could hide away from what he and Insa had created in their quest to become gods. High in Adeqor's domed tower, where not even time could kill him. Sera and him were happy there. He had almost forgotten. *Almost...* Until the comet appeared in the sky that night. He would have to face his work one last time. To find out if it was all worth it. So, he walked through the busy streets. Past the entrances to the slave mines, barricaded over with debris; past burning houses and temples; burning people on stakes. Acrid fumes of seared flesh and charred bone reminded Adeqor of his work with Insa and made his stomach turn. He covered his mouth and nose to stem the smell, but it did nothing.

Adeqor arrived to find Insa's home had been ransacked. The crystal windows were shattered, the heavy whiteoak door wide open. Adeqor walked in and saw the gaping mouths of empty chests yawning at him. The breeze scuffled loose papers around the floor. Cupboards and shelves were empty. But the bookshelf sat mostly untouched. *Insa always swore it would be safe. "The enslaved and smallfolk never touch the books,"* he had said. *"They think they're full of hexes. And you know, they are not totally wrong!"*

Adeqor walked over to the bookshelf, his bare feet slapping on the hardwood floors. He chewed a fingernail as he scanned the names of the volumes on the shelf. *There's a Word for That* by Yeru Mori; *Discipline Your Slave* by Ictetus; and *The Purple Cloak for Beginners* by Aesop, until he found the one he was looking for. *The Truth* by Insa Rolin. He ran his finger up the old spine, then pulled it out. The bookshelf swung inwards to reveal a narrow stairway. *"No one wants the real truth Adee,"* Insa had said. *"Only their own version of it. One they're comfortable with believing."*

Adeqor followed an unnatural, flickering red light down the stairs to the bottom. A man stood alone at the back of a large room and made no notice of Adeqor. The walls were lined with Human-like creatures in glass tubes. They were floating in a thick liquid, each with a different level of transparency. Adeqor looked at one with webbed fingers and toes. The thing opened its glowing green eyes that were all too Human, and Adeqor almost shit himself. The creature had gills on its neck and mouthed the word "*help*" in the common tongue. Adeqor turned his head away. In a tall, thin cage along the other wall was a wolf-like creature standing upright. It had the chest of an elk and the paws of a bear. Adeqor noticed chafed and bare skin where its chains were too tight. As it drooled a greenish saliva, Adeqor could see the points of jagged fangs. *You've gone too far, Insa... you've created too much. Too much...*

The man at the back of the room hadn't even looked up from the naked body on the table.

"*Insa.*" Adeqor trembled, angry at himself for revealing his fear. The man lifted his head slowly. He turned around, gazing at Adeqor with gaunt, colourless eyes and jagged cheekbones.

"Who is it?" Insa said. His eyes were protruding from his skull and bloodshot. His skin was as pale as milk.

"It's me. Adeqor. Have I changed so much already?" Adeqor looked down at his frail body, frowning. Insa stared at him with those maddened eyes, and Adeqor finally saw recognition there.

"Adeqor?"

"I needed to see how our work turned out."

"Turned out?" Insa seemed confused. Like he'd forgotten where Adeqor fit into all of this.

"Did you speak with Them? Did They come?" Adeqor asked. Insa's straight face slowly twisted into a demented grin. He laughed like he was choking on worms.

"Come? Adeqor, They stand before you right now. I am one of *Them.*" Insa's eyes were mad with passion. It filled Adeqor with horror. "When the star falls, I will Descend from this body and become a Creator. Karaat has told it true."

Insa turned back to the body in front of him. *He's lost his mind to the work. The madness of Creation has soiled him...* Together, he and Insa had created many non-human beings. Mostly to push the limits of what was possible with their magics, but partly to gain *Their* attention. He and Insa only wanted to prove Warlocks, too, were god-like; that they, too, could conjure divine creation.

The Creators had fallen into the earth a million moons ago, and the Sorcerers were their creation. When the Sorcerers created the Warlocks—a race superior to all of Nature's children—they were gifted descension, invited to meet their makers. The Sorcerers built the grand empire of Yehven in divine honour to their gods before their departure. And if Yehven was Empress, the city of Ailar was her shining gold crown. Then, one day, the Warlocks of old awoke into a world where their makers had gone. After inheriting such power as was left to them, it didn't take long for the first of the Warlocks to subjugate the races of Nature in hopes of meeting the same divine end as the Sorcerers. It was the dream of the Yehvenki Empire to gain Their attention. To show the Creators that Yehven had reached the same mastery that the Sorcerers had. The Yehvenki worshipped the Creator God, Karaat, and made him so strong through their worship that his Words became the most powerful weapon ever known. But the Creators only took and never gave. They stole dreams and ate hope. And the Warlocks pushed further and further to impress Them. With every land that the Yehvenki Empire conquered and every culture they indoctrinated, Karaat grew stronger from the people's growing worship. His Words grew stronger, and the magics of Yehven became godly. Nature had been usurped.

Insa turned to one of his tables and grabbed a long serrated knife. When he stepped away, Adeqor could see the true, horrific nature of what his old friend was doing to that corpse. It wasn't a corpse at all. It was *alive.* Its bluish pale chest rose and fell from slow breaths. Insa had used black magics to keep it alive. Then Adeqor saw why. Something was moving underneath the clammy skin of the victim.

"What have you done, Insa?"

"The Human body is the best incubator I have found. It keeps the wyrm larvae at the exact right temperature to grow," Insa said proudly. "Of course, the hard part is getting them *out.* Haha!"

Adeqor shook his head. The blue skin of the body was moving and writhing all over. Things were *crawling* around beneath its skin.

"What have you done, Insa?"

"I am a Creator, Adeqor. I am a God, and I created something worthy. A race that could even rival *us. Draku.* "

"Kill this thing, Insa. Get rid of it, now. Fight this madness. You can still die with the honour you once had. Die as the Insa I knew and loved." Adeqor was pleading. His eyes had welled with tears at the thought of all the years he'd spent beside this man. He had become a brother to him. Family.

Insa laughed madly, his face twisted in rapture.

"This is not the first, anyway. It would make no difference to be rid of this one. I was only trying to make them *better.* "

"You made more than one."

"How else would they reproduce?"

"*Reproduce?* Insa, you've gone mad."

"Maybe I have."

"Where did you hide them?"

"Across the Old Sea. In the wild lands of Ardura. They will be safe there. They can *live* there. Start anew. The funny thing about these, you see." Insa called a spirit of Fire, and the body ignited in black, smoking flame. It writhed in spasms, but it wasn't dying. The thing on the table screamed, and not in pain as it should be, but in some kind of twisted, horrible joy—its eyes wide and mouth gaping like a minstrel making strange faces at children. "They drink fire like water, Adee, and they can never die."

"You've cursed those lands with monsters, Insa. You've brought a blight on all of us."

"Cursed? I think not. What I created was no curse," Insa said.

Adeqor shook his head in disbelief. How could he be angry at him? He'd fallen into the same madness years ago. Together, Adeqor and Insa had created one non-Human beast after the other. He was absolutely ashamed that they had used blood magics. *Abused* blood magics. Always hoping one day the Creators would Ascend to praise their work, that Karaat, the Creator God, would take them down, away from these frail, near useless bodies.

They always felt like they needed more. More creations. More victims to test with. Adeqor resorted to using his own slave's family to do their testing on. *Your own family. Don't forget the truth, no matter how ugly.* Nine had never forgiven him for turning his sister—their sister—into that... hideous failed creation. It was a vile, horrible thing. When Adeqor realized how far he'd gone, he walked away from Insa and never came back. He went into his self-imposed exile. Unable to face himself or his work any longer. *But this... this was worse than even that.*

Suddenly, Adeqor remembered why he had come.

"Sera and I are going below. I came to offer you a spot. The Ailaryan Order allows one guest," said Adeqor. Insa stared at him with disdain. *He's looking at you like you're an insect buzzing in his ear.*

"The Ailaryan Order?"

"Eralis has overthrown Creon's New Order initiative. The Rulers of Yehven will all die in the starfall. The comet will take them all. He's made sure of it."

Insa seemed unbothered by anything Adeqor said. "And what would Sera think of you using your guest spot on a madman?"

"She will be fine with it," Adeqor lied.

Insa studied the body. His grey hair was matted with grease and flecked with dandruff. His face was sunken in and pale and his hands were shaking. There was a time Adeqor looked up at Insa from a place of similar decay and begged for his help. Insa had told him there was no help. That Adeqor just simply wasn't strong enough to handle the work of gods. *And how have you handled it, old friend?* The person before him was not the same man Adeqor once knew and loved. That man was full of life and wonder. He was beaming with hope. *This is not Insa Rolin. This is a poisoned husk of that man.*

Insa gave a wicked smile, revealing crippled, yellowed teeth below his thin lips. "I can't leave my work. Not until the very last. Let the Abori breach the walls. Let the star fall. It makes no difference to me." Insa raised his hands to the ceiling. "We *knew* the Abori would come if we went too far. We *knew* they would bring the Starfall when Karaat's Words reached apex. The warnings are everywhere, the Sorcerers wove them into everything."

With a stride, he stood in front of Adeqor. "But how could we ever know what we were capable of, *truly* capable of, without exploring the *full* power of Karaat? The power of gods?"

"Stop this," Adeqor said, stumbling back.

"It can never stop, can't you see? When the Sorcerers vanished, the Yehvenki spread the Words of Karaat across the entire globe. He is worshipped on every continent and praised upon every sunrise and sunfell. The Sorcerers warned against it, and we ignored the warnings. And the Words have never been stronger. We are as strong as gods, now, Adee. We have become Them." Insa took a step closer, pressing Adeqor against a bookshelf with ease. "Nature has come to claim back her land, but we don't need her anymore."

Adeqor's breath was knocked out of him, but that wasn't what hurt most. Some repulsive instinct was stirring inside of him—a kind of bittersweet melancholy. He was broken as he realized his meeting with Insa was going to end badly. *Just leave. Get back to Sera.* Adeqor had held hope that Insa had made some deal with the Creators to save him from the Starfall. Maybe he knew something that could get them out of all of this. Adeqor had extended that hope to believing Insa would forgive him and take him and Sera with him if he *had* found a way out.

No gods are going to save you. Insa will not save you.

"It's over, Adee. This is the end." Insa's eyes were yellow-red and glazed with lust. "The Abori will exterminate us and ours so that none survive. Don't you see, they know about the tunnels, Adee, they know. The Abori have risen a stairway to Hell and are coming to throw us down head first. Mage, they call her. She sings sweet songs of Starfall and everwinter. This is the end, Adee, go." Insa clutched a vile of something ink-black from the table behind him and swallowed its contents. The body behind him writhed below char-blackened skin as the flames smoked out. Insa's black lips curled into some kind of wicked grin that made Adeqor's stomach sour. *Who is this? What can become of a man?*

Footsteps coming down the stairs made Adeqor scurry back like a scared rat. Four Golden Guards came into the basement, one after another. The guards all smiled drunken grins and the rank stench of them stung Adeqor's nose. *You didn't close the bookshelf. Imbecile.* The dull light in Insa's dank chamber wasn't enough for Adeqor to see their ears.

"Why are you doing this?" Adeqor cried. He cursed himself for letting fear slip in his words.

"What else would you expect us to do?" The guard pointed her jagged spear at Insa. "We thought it'd be better if no one made it to the tunnels—if we all just got burned up together, eh?"

Insa glared into her and, like a minstrel, he laughed a maddened cackle. Adeqor watched horror grab ahold of the guard and freeze her to the spot in the same way as him. Insa held his arms out wide as his eyes began to fill with blackness. He began to speak in ancient tongues before his voice broke into something more like rushing water than words.

The guard's terror leaked out of her like a kettle as she screamed and thrust her spear right into Insa's gut, who did nothing to stop it. He only continued to laugh as blood pooled around him. His eyes were as black as krakens.

Then, he whispered in a voice so deep it could have only come from below, *"Karaat,"* until his eyes went blank as snow.

The guards were inspecting the corpse laid out on the table with a sour look on their faces.

"What the fuck is this?" one guard said to another. And with a Word, Adeqor brought the ceiling down on them.

One guard had missed the debris and came to Adeqor with his spear lowered. Adeqor noticed the guard hadn't been Kissed. Adeqor smiled and blew his eardrums open with a whisper. *The power of Karaat is still at its height on this day. His Words will ring out another symphony with force. This will not be His Last Ballad.*

Adeqor studied the glass tubes and cages—the beasts his partner had created. They were prisoners here, like folk in a dungeon. Insa had gone too far. All of them, the whole race of Warlocks, had gone too far. *We are not gods. We are birds that have flown too high, and now we must watch as the sky burns us up and sends us falling back down to where we came from, a husk of burning feathers.*

Adeqor took Insa's notebook, a worn volume filled with Words that could shape a world for better or for worse. Insa had kept every secret of Yehven in this book, distilled into Words that he could use to shape a New World. Words that he could use to become a *God*. The book was bound in Human leather and tied with a single string, but magics would keep it from ever falling apart.

Then the guard's words echoed in Adeqor's mind. *We've had enough of the masters.* The guards were rebelling. They would surely go to his tower to kill *him*, just as they've done with every other master. *Sera. Sera is in danger.*

He clutched the ragged volume close to his chest as he ran back through the city.

The star was screaming as it tore through the sky. The sound was all-encompassing. It was all there was. The sound and the movement of his body. He could hear many guards behind him. Following him. He kept moving.

The foyer to the glass towers were still empty but for the body of the man Adeqor killed on his way out. His lungs felt like they were filled with honey, and his legs and knees would not carry him any farther. He sat down on the base of the stairs, heaving for breath. *Sera. She is all you have left. She is all there is.* He wanted so badly to love like he used to. He wanted so badly for his heart to heal from the madness that broke it. He turned and ran as fast as his legs would take him up the stairs. As he slowed, he could hear guards running up the stairs further down behind him. When he burst into his room through the whiteoak doors, he took a deep breath. Sera was there, just as she had been before he left.

"What's wrong?" she asked. She looked worried. She had no idea what was going on.

"The guards are revolting. The enslaved, too." Adeqor was still puffing for a breath. He hadn't run in so many years. As he held Sera and the fear of losing her washed away, another pain suddenly hit him. *You should have apologized to Nine. For what you did to his—our—sister. They were all each other had in this world and you destroyed that. The father you three shared was nobody. Your mother was somebody, and that's the only difference between you and them. Have you forgotten that that is the only difference?* He and Nine were so alike that it scared Adeqor, and he denied it by holding himself above Nine. *His name is not Nine. Can you not even call him by his real name? Is he just a number to you?* All these years he had wanted to apologize and never did. The thought inserted itself to the forefront of his mind now that it was too late.

Sera frowned. "They're coming, Adee, what will they do to us?"

Adeqor just chewed his fingernail. Sera held her hands to her head.

"Yora came by again. She said Grand Emperor Creon jumped from his balcony. It's all gone to plan, Adee. The New Order has overthrown the old. The betrayal worked. Only the *clean* Warlocks will make it below."

"We're going to make it, dear. But we have to go now, and we will have to fight, Sera. We have to go if we would go," Adeqor said. But there was already a thumping in the stairwell. Adeqor could hear dozens of guards outside the whiteoak door. *If you leave this room the guards will kill you. If you stay, the tunnels will close and you'll be stardust.*

"There is nowhere for us to go, Adee. We waited too long." Sera looked at him with tears streaming down her face. Adeqor remembered the day they married. He'd promised to love and protect her. *But promises mean nothing to you, do they? Your love faded as the magics became more clear. You gave up love for long life with Insa's spell. But what is one without the other? Misery? Solitude?* Adeqor pulled Sera close. He wanted so badly to love her like he once did and so he acted.

"They can't get in, Sera. We can stay here together. We can leave this world together," he said. "Look at me." She looked at him. Beautiful brown eyes staring back at him. They used to make his heart flutter. He longed for that feeling more than anything. "The Soma," he said. Her eyes brightened. They wouldn't let the guards or the star take them. They would slip away into a drug-induced coma with smiles on their faces. Sera's chest quivered as she let herself sob. Adeqor sobbed with her, gripping her face with both hands and breathing her in. This was it. He gathered two vials three quarters full of Soma and handed one to Sera.

Then there was a rumbling sound from behind them.

"Hey." A voice. It was their servant, Nine. He had appeared from behind the fireplace. Adeqor had forgotten there was an entrance there; it was so filthy he had never minded to use it. "This way. Follow me," said Nine.

"Thank Karaat, Sera. We're saved." Adeqor said, gripping Insa's notebook tight beneath one arm. Sera smiled hopefully. And the three of them disappeared down a dark tunnel.

THE SLAVE

Six Hours to Starfall

"WE'LL NEVER REALLY DIE!" Mose shouted as he raised the glass goblet to the sky. "We'll live forever as legends!" The conglomerate of Golden Guards and Ailaryan enslaved bellowed out a mad cheer. "You've got nothing left to lose now. Not with that star falling. I'm here to take you through to the other side of Hell!" He was reciting jargon from the books of Oliander. More cheers. *They cheered for Oliander, too. Oh, yes.*

He wondered how much basilisk blood was too much. *A dab to deafen and a dram to kill. Be careful, be careful to hold them still.* The old children's song rang in his head.

The aristocrats would never hear them down here. Not from up in their towers. Mose pointed his finger at one of the Golden Guards and beckoned him forth. The guard nodded and knelt before Mose. His golden armour was as thin as the threadbare shirt Mose arrived at the Glass Towers in but was as strong as a solid stone wall—the magics made it so. The masters carved each guard's armour in the Words of power that best suited them. They had carved this one with strength and cunning.

"What's your name, brother?" Mose asked.

"Marton," he trembled.

Mose had seen this one before—alone, quiet. *This one is a coward. And he's scared. But a great truth lies in fear, and he's living in that truth now. No one is more brave than who was once a coward.*

"You'll never grow old, Marton. This is the last day of your life. What do you want from it?" Mose said.

"I want to give my life for your cause. I want to do something worthwhile before I die," Marton said. "I want the masters to suffer." His voice was still trembling. He took off his golden helm and pulled his long black hair away from his ear.

"You're not giving your life." Mose gathered Marton's hair in both hands and tied it into a knot. "You're taking it back. Can't you see? It's not until you welcome death that you are truly free to do anything," Mose said, frowning. He swirled the basilisk blood in the glass goblet. The acidity of it burned the back of his throat. "You're finally going to live like there is no tomorrow. Every meal you eat today will be immaculate. You will savour every breath. You are truly free now, Marton." Mose poured the blood into the guard's ear. This guard was strong, the carvings on his armour made him so, but even the Words couldn't stop that kind of pain, and it wasn't long before he started screaming. The guards and slaves of the rebellion cheered and chanted.

"The New World!"

Screams of pain bellowed out in the lower halls of the towers of the aristocrats as Mose filled the ears of dozens upon dozens of rebels with acid. Screams and cheers to balance them out. Those were the sounds of rebellion.

Marton handed Mose another goblet full of acid, still reeling from his Kiss, by the look of distress in his eyes. The acid would deafen them to the Words. It would give them *some* resistance. And even *some,* when the masters expect none, could be enough to make them question their own strength. *Enough to let them know they aren't gods. So when the star falls on them, they know that the filth beneath their feet rose and stood eye to eye as equals, if but only for one glorious moment.*

"Each of us will kill our masters today," Mose screamed, loud enough that every rebel in agony would feel his voice vibrate through them. "Each of us will obtain their identity key. Afterwards, we gather at the entrance to the tunnels." Mose basked in the revelry erupting around him. "If everything goes according to plan, I will have the key to open the doorway. Only the most elite Warlocks are welcome in the tunnels, so there shouldn't be more than a few hundred of them. Once we're in, we will have to kill every person in there. It will be bloody, and many of us will die."

The rebels cheered. Mose had trained them well. These folks didn't fear death anymore. They feared dying without ever really living. They feared their lives were meaningless. But Mose offered them meaning.

"The new world will be ours!" Mose let all of his passion flow out of him. His flesh flared up with goosebumps. This was the most thrill he'd ever felt. He had carefully planned this rebellion for years and never thought he'd actually make it work. The comet in the sky gave him his opportunity. It gave him enough chaos to climb.

"The sun is rising, Mose." Marton wiped tears from under his eyes as he spoke. Mose nodded. His master would rise with the sun and soon be calling out for breakfast. Mose had to answer that call to avoid any suspicion. *We've come too far to be sloppy now. Patience will win this battle, much more than any conventional wisdom.*

"Bear this pain with pride. The Kiss of Silence is a sacred ritual amongst the Abori. Only the standouts amongst standouts wear the Kiss. This is your moment. Be thankful to actually *feel* something of substance for the first time in your life. A meaningful sacrifice. This is your badge of honour. A kiss from death. A reminder." Mose raised his hand to bid his rebels farewell. They cheered for him. *This... this is what you've always deserved. Admiration. It only took the sky ripping open...*

With the growing adulation at his back, Mose made his way up through the lower levels of the Glass Towers. Up and up, the stairs winded. Then Mose heard footsteps coming down. *Fuck...* The masters didn't allow the enslaved to be in this stairwell. They didn't allow them to be anywhere except outside of their master's door. Mose stood still. *Think...* The footsteps got closer, and he could only think to grab the small knife he'd tucked into his belt. The person rounded the corner. Mose immediately saw the purple of his cloak. *Fuck.* It was master Dante. Dante's eyes flicked open.

"What are you doing here? You're not supposed to be here!" Dante shouted. Mose had no choice but to dive at him with his knife. Dante shouted a Word, but it was sloppy, his voice was too panicked, and Mose stabbed him in the gut before he could speak a Word again. Twice, thrice, four times, five the blade pierced soft flesh. And over and over Mose let the lust of hate take over. *You take and you take, and now you will feel what it's like to be taken from.* Saliva hung from his mouth as Mose turned feral in his aggression. Finally, he stopped himself when he realized blood spatter covered his clothes. He pulled himself away, peering at the dead person bleeding out in the stairwell, disgusted. *Sloppy, sloppy.* He had no time to wash now. He left the body and ran up the steps.

It grew colder and colder as he ascended until, finally, Mose stood in the outside halls of his master's apartments. The glass dome of his chamber nearly kissed the clouds. The aristocrats stayed cool up there while the rest sweltered below—each of their glass chambers sprouting from the side of the main tower like mushrooms. Exotic tapestries from Gwelar, Arish Pura, Si'tan, and everywhere else a Yehvenki ship could probe and propagate adorned the walls. Mose stood outside of the thick, immaculately carved whiteoak door and waited. *Patience. Just a few more hours, and he will finally know your pain.*

Mose had waited many long years for his chance at revenge. He had spent many long nights awake with the cries of his young sister echoing through his mind. Mose had promised her he would always protect her. But he couldn't protect her from his own brother. When their master took her for one of his experiments, Mose had had a choice to make. Do something, *anything,* to save his sister, then his master would have killed him and still performed experiments on Mose's sister. Or, he could watch them carry his sister away and back again in chains, her body limp and broken, but alive. That was all he had wanted—to keep her alive. That was why he brought Cleo here, to the Glass Towers, after their father died.

"We should go west, Mose, away from here," Cleo had said, her eyes red and swollen.

"We can have a better life if we find our mother, Cleo. Look." Mose had pointed to the Glass Towers, his hands still stained with the same dirt that covered his father's cold body. Cleo's face lit up with wonder at the sight of the silver shafts rising up to the pink twilit clouds. It wasn't much of a choice at all. It was the Glass Towers or death. He had never imagined their mother would be dead, too, and instead of love, they would be met with the son of their mother and treated as filth beneath his feet. *You did that to Cleo. You brought her here...*

When Adeqor and his guards had dragged Cleo away that final night, Mose had thought that she would come back alive as she always did. Broken was better than dead.

But she didn't come back. Mose stared at the chips in the stone caused by his sister struggling. The small indents were nagging re-minders of what had happened. Mose had spent hundreds upon hundreds of hours staring at those chips outside his master's—his brother's— door, remembering. He could still hear her screams. *They called her Ten. Ten, as if she was nothing but a number. Her name was Cleo. She was your sister, you fucking monster. I'm your brother. What is wrong with you? Why are you forcing me to kill you?* The sound of the Golden Guard knocking Mose's sister uncon-scious with his gold-plated fist; the sound of the steel chains around her wrists and ankles dragging across the cold stone floor; the sound of her voice cracking beneath a desperate scream—these memories lived in Mose's head like night coloured moths that never ceased to stop fluttering.

"Nine!" Mose's master called out and snapped him out of it. *My name is Mose. Soon you will see I am more than just a number, master.* Mose took a deep breath. *A few more hours and you'll have your vengeance. This is your last hour as Nine. Put on a smile and don't raise any suspicion.* Mose opened the door, curious to see what his master wanted for his last breakfast.

"Hold it still," Mose complained. Marton was struggling to hold the pot of sauce below Mose's cock without looking.

"I'm trying."

"Just turn around and look at the thing, guy. It's just a cock," Mose said. Marton turned around, peering through squinted eyes, and held the pot steady. "There we go." Mose continued to piss in the golden cream sauce and sighed in relief. He'd been saving this one up.

"What's the point of this, if you're going to kill him, anyway?" Marton asked as Mose shook out the last few drops.

"It's principle, Marton. This is what happens when you stoke the fires of rebellion. When you piss on those below you, they piss back sometimes," Mose said.

"Yes, of course." Marton bowed like Mose was some kind of prophet. Sweat soaked Marton's body dripping from his forehead;

both of his eyes were twitching. Common side effects of searing your eardrums shut with acid. "Alright, give it here."

Mose set the poached quail eggs on a fresh half loaf with honey-glazed tomatoes drizzled in an extra special cream of pearl on a tray. He removed a small vial from the inside pocket of his cloak and uncorked the top. He shuddered as the smell of it burned his nose, and he poured a small draught of the stuff into the Soma wine. It was oil pressed from petals of the harrisene flower. It was vibrantly red and as smooth and thick as butter, but flowed like water. Consuming the flower whole does nothing, the petals are its poison's own remedy, but its oils will cause a slow acting paralysis if ingested. *It's too easy.* Mose grinned. Generations of Yehvenki masters had lived and died with the Words of obedience falling from the clouds. There was never a worry that the enslaved might fight back. They couldn't even imagine it. When they thought of betrayal, they only thought of other masters. Only the rich could eat the rich in this world.

But when the comet appeared in the sky and the Singers left the pyramids, they freed the weight of obedience from Mose's shoulders. Something came alive in him. Something long suppressed by magics. He felt it growing inside of him like springtime in his soul. A power that he had never felt. The strength and freedom to right what has wronged him. He found the courage to fight back, and he shouted that message as loud as he could to all who would hear it. And it was as contagious as the bloody plague.

Mose took the tray and headed for his master's apartments. He dropped it off, and Adeqor and Sera barely noticed him. That was typical. He was filth. An enslaved man from Meylara. He and his sister were orphans, left in the streets when they were young. Mose was a Meylarran street rat, just like his father. Not a pure-blooded

Ailaryan, like his mother. *They'll notice you as you stand over them and watch them suffer their last breaths, though.* Mose was beaming. They couldn't stop him. He had always known he would do something great. He had always known one day he would get the last laugh in all of this.

Mose left his masters' apartments and made his way up the stairs of the Glass Towers towards the very top.

He was going to kill the Emperor of Yehven.

Three Hours to Starfall

"I CAN'T GO THROUGH with this, Mose," Myril sighed. He paced back and forth, holding his sword in hand. Crow's feet stretched out from his eyes in deep wrinkles. *This hurts him more than it hurts you... he's concerned you've gone mad...* Myril was one of the only people who showed Mose and his sister love in these towers. Myril was a true friend and more of a brother than Mose's actual brother. But Myril's master was the imperial hand that held the only key to the Emperor's chamber. "If you try to survive down there in the tunnels with this crew of repressed peoples, it won't end well for you. They harbour too much hate. It will come out when the food runs low. There will be another rebellion below, and there will be no way to manipulate that one. This won't play out like you plan. Just die in peace, Mose. Let it go," Myril pleaded.

Mose scoffed. *Let it go?* He hadn't come this far to let it go. *Let it go? No. That can't happen.* "Just give me the key, Myril. The blood is already on your hands. Your master is dead."

"What is killing the Emperor going to do for you? I don't want to take this any further, Mose. I don't need Karaat's judgement upon me before I go down. My master deserved to die. He was a twisted, perverted fuck. But Creon has done nothing to sleight me. He's been a decent emperor to us. Ailar has never been more wealthy. I have no right under the eyes of Karaat to claim vengeance against him."

Mose shook his head. *Ailar has never been so greedy, so stained.*

"You really can't see, can you? We're going to send a message to Karaat. All these years of being enslaved to our masters, and He did nothing to save us. But we can rise and save ourselves. Killing Creon will make us worthy of the Great God's notoriety. It will prove that we are not lesser." Mose felt the tears well in his eyes, and he let them slide down his cheek. He truly loved Myril. He'd been a dear friend to Mose for many years. But Mose would kill him for the key to the Emperor's chamber if it came to that. The thought of it made the tears fall faster.

"You've never known when to quit, eh? Why can't you just accept death, Mose? That star is the only sign from Karaat we should pay attention to. It's time to stop. Just lay down and die in peace. Our race has abused this power for too long. The Earth is fighting back against us, now. We cannot fight Nature any longer, Mose, can't you see? We cannot control what is not ours. It's over," Myril said. He raised the sword. Mose sighed. He didn't want to have to use the Words so soon.

"I'm sorry, Myril," Mose said. Myril rushed at him with the sword. "Ventes," Mose sang. *Destroy.* And the moment the Word left his tongue, Myril's head melted away from his body and splattered all over the floor like bloody mud.

Mose's fingers were tingling. His heart thumped in his chest like a bell. He was breathing heavily, like he'd just had an orgasm. The thrill of the Word was rushing through him. He relished in it. His eyes rolled into the back of his head at the thought of saying another Word.

Mose looked around, longing for someone, anyone, to catch him so he'd have to kill them, too. But nobody came. He had heard his master use the Word time and time again to rid himself of documents or other garbage. He had practiced mouthing it, letting it soar around in his mind like a golden eagle. He could never have imagined it feeling so good—*tasting* so good.

Mose walked over to the body of his dead friend and fished through his white cloak. But there was no key. He pulled out a scroll instead. He unrolled it. There were only a couple of Words written on it. Irill tur Sa'illes. *Speak true and enter.* Mose realized then that the key to the Emperor's chamber wasn't a key, but a Word. He tucked it away into his pocket and wept as he said a prayer to Karaat to guide Myril's soul safely to Hell.

Two Hours to Starfall

THE EMPEROR'S CHAMBER WAS its own palace. Mose walked beneath grand arches of diamond-studded marble, between pillars of alabaster carved with likenesses of Karaat, to an antechamber lined with stone heads of various shapes placed neatly on pillars of solid jet. They were uneven, carved by different sculptors. Each head came from a statue of worship and represented a dead god that the Empire had destroyed. Above each head hung the flag of the people who once believed in them. These were the Emperor's trophies. These were Karaat's dinner scraps. Through the antechamber was Creon's leisure room.

Mose walked in and couldn't believe what he saw. Glass dome ceilings gave a frightening view of the comet. It was the only thing in the sky now—a glowing mass of black descending from the grey clouds. Dim morning light radiated from behind, casting the room with an eerie glow.

Creon swung gently from a noose in the centre of the massive theatre. His purple cloak hung loosely off one shoulder. Mose held his hands to his mouth. *Someone else got to him first... that, or he was a damn coward and couldn't face the tunnels.* Mose felt his body weighed down with disappointment. He was hoping for a meaningful sacrifice for the revolution. A prominent symbol that his rebels could stand behind. And here, the Great Emperor of Ailar died alone in his palace.

But something wasn't right. There was no sign of the rest of his family. The emperor had a wife and three children. That's when Mose noticed a strange book opened on a lectern beneath Creon. Glass jars and tubes, some empty, some full of strange liquids, leaked across the tables and floor. It smelled of sorcery. A book, its pages yellow with age, was written in a strange language, some eldritch tongue echoing back into eternity. Mose couldn't read it, but he recognized one symbol sketched below a block of text. It was the

Yehvenki surgeon's symbol for the soul. *This bastard pulled some dark sorcery...* The air stunk of sulphur and vinegar—of madness. Strange sounds lingered in the darkness. The emperor had summoned something to take his soul to another time; another place. And the stench of the beast that took him still lingered. It was unnatural. *This was a disgrace of an emperor. He sold his soul to sorcery...*

Mose couldn't have it. This was *his* moment. He untied Creon and let his stiff body drop to the floor. Mose shuddered as Creon's head cracked on the marble floors. He dragged Creon's corpse to the balcony. Mose decided Creon weighed about half as much as a pyramid. It took him a great heave to get Creon's body upright. He used the railing as leverage to slide the cold body onto the ledge. After that, Creon's corpse flopped over the railing like it couldn't wait to go for a soar. Mose watched as the fleshy thing that used to be the Grand Emperor of Yehven fall, getting smaller and smaller until he disappeared out of sight. Mose imagined he made quite a smack down there. It would send the message to his followers that the rebellion had begun. It would send a different, more disturbing message to everyone else, and that was what really made Mose smile—that this was well and truly the end, and no god or emperor would be saving them from the hell to come. *Fear for your lives as Cleo feared for hers.*

The raucous comet was ripping through the sky like thunder. It looked to be thrice the size of the sun now. Mose couldn't help but stare at it. *You would have loved this, Cleo, my sweet sister—this lullaby in your honour amidst the sound of starfall. The Golden City is ours. The world is ours, if but only for a moment.* Mose's gaze drifted downwards. Beyond the city gates, there was a mass of Abori warriors. Yehvenki soldiers were defending the walls, but Mose didn't think they would last much longer. Soon, the Abori would breach these walls. The Yehvenki population would get what they deserved. Mose, even though his blood was diluted by filth, had the nightmares of Warlocks, too. He had seen it all happen. The Kiss of Silence. Scalping and flaying of eyelids. The Abori would butcher them and tie the rest up to watch the sky fall on them. This was extermination. But not before the Abori brought humility down upon them. Not before the Abori taught them their place amongst Nature.

This empire has gone too far. But if I was a Creator, it would be different. It would be better. Mose licked his lips and tasted the Word on the tip of his tongue. *I would be a better god than mine.*

One Hour to Starfall

MOSE HURRIED BACK TO his master's chamber. He could only pray that there was no suspicion. That there were no accidents. He only had one thing left to do now. To kill Adeqor and Sera, get their identity keys, and open the doors of the tunnels for the guards. Whether he survived the massacre that followed would be the will of Karaat. Cries bounced off the walls as he ran through the tower halls. *Please don't be too late.*

He hurried up the winding stairs to the upper floors. He stopped when he heard screaming. The soft clink of golden boots coming down the stairs sent Mose running back down. He couldn't risk these guards being loyalists. It was likely the guards were fighting each other at this point. Mose slid into an open chamber door. Two masters, husband and wife, were laid out on the floor in a pool of dark red blood. Killed by their own slaves or guards. Mose crawled into their fireplace and felt around the back. A trap door connected every fireplace in the Glass Towers to a tunnel system. The masters of long ago had built it for moments just like this. These days, most of the masters were ignorant of them. And the ones who knew never used them because of how run down and dirty they were.

Mose pushed open the trapdoor and crawled in. He emerged in a dark hallway covered in soot and cobwebs. He brushed himself off and carried on down the dark hallway, dragging his hand along one wall for navigation. Feeling the runes carved by the Sorcerers, who built the Glass Towers back when the skies were different. Mose imagined that they believed these Towers would be here forever after they left.

He tried to keep his bearings as he walked. Moving north, then west until he found a stairwell. Once he was in the upper hallways, he knew the path. He found the doorway that led into Sera and Adeqor's chamber and opened it up. The fireplace slid forward, and Mose pushed it to the side. Adeqor and Sera were standing there in plain sight. Holding each other desperately. Looking terrified and hopeless. *Perfect.*

"Hey," Mose came out of the fireplace. "This way, follow me."

Adeqor and Sera looked at Mose like he was a god. *Admiration. This is what you deserve.*

"Thank Karaat, Sera. We're saved," Adeqor said, and they followed Mose into the dark hallway.

THE GOLDEN GUARD

One Hour to Starfall

MARTON WAS TREMBLING FROM the thrill. The magics still lingered at the tip of his tongue. The Words were like wine. *No, better than that. Better than...* He couldn't imagine anything better than wine. His life had very few thrills. His ears were still buzzing with the sting of acid, and he winced when he tried to scratch them.

The dead masters laid on the ground. The chamber's pink veined marble floor was painted with pieces of Yora's head. Ren lay beside her, his lifeblood still draining from his neck. *You did that. Feeble minded you... with but a Word.* By Marton's own doing. *With nothing but a Word.* The thought of breaking down immovable obstacles was one that made Marton uneasy. The empire had whipped and cut the ambition out of him when he was young. He was afraid to leave his station. He was afraid to rise above and lose everything he already had. *If even I can use these magics, the world is well and truly lost.* But still, he plucked the identity stones from around his former masters' necks and tucked them away with a smile on his face.

Yora and Ren had been decent masters. They kept Marton fed and gave him new clothing every month. And so Marton served them and served the empire without question. The empire had even given his mom and sister a house. *And Lyanna even lived in it for a short while...* Still Marton couldn't forget the pain he'd seen in his mom's face when Bazal took him away to the Glass Towers. The pain in her eyes when the cattle wayns carried Lyanna's body away. Marton looked down upon his former masters and spat on Yora's corpse.

He walked back out into the chaotic streets. Fellow guards with blank eyes gawked on either side of him. No blood on their hands, but something darker stained their souls now. Once a person spoke the Words, they could never stop. The Words take over. Marton nodded at one of them, who nodded back. The deeds had been done. They had been Kissed by Silence. The rebellion had started.

Marton walked towards the tunnels, carved into the cliff face by the Sorcerers when the skies were new. The tunnels went deep below the earth, and the Yehvenki had built palaces inside to survive the darkness the Starfall would bring. Marton had done his part. He had earned his place amongst the rebellion by killing his master. He had the identity stone as proof. All he needed to do was show Mose his master's key and Mose would permit him in. *As long as Mose completed his task unharmed.* There was always the risk of death in rebellion.

He'd never dreamed this revenge was possible, but he had tasted it and imagined it for so long it felt like a dream. To take the life of the one who took so much from him. He did not ask to be castrated at thirteen and given the golden chest plate carved with Words of power and cunning. He did not ask and he did not desire it, but they were the gifts that the Yehvenki Empire gave to him and forced him to accept them, and be grateful.

As a boy, Marton watched his mother work all night to extract oil from the eucalyptus leaves she had gathered all day. She would then infuse the oil with mint leaves and sell it at sunrise down at the purple docks where the aristocrats buy their soaps and beauty tinctures. At the end of it all, she barely got enough coin to keep Marton from starving. Every time he had gone to the market with her, he had wanted to scream at the rich folk bartering, ignorant in their velvet robes. *"Oh, I don't quite think it's worth a whole star, darling. I'll give you half a sphinx."* When his mom accepted the deals that bordered on robbery, Marton pulled on her shirt. *"Mom, that was less than half of what it's worth,"* Marton had said. His mother smiled like she did when she was telling Marton and Lyanna stories. Her eyes squinted and dimples formed in her cheeks. She knelt down to brush the hair from his eyes. She always got down on his level to tell him important things. *"You cannot bite the hand that feeds, son. You must learn that life is like love—sometimes, something is better than nothing. We choose our own happiness, Marton. These aristocrats make their own rules. But one day, judgement will come, and we will be on the proper side of it. They can break our bodies through overwork and malnutrition, but they can never break our minds or our hearts. We will safeguard those with everything we have."*

Repression forced Marton to stand by and watch as the masters depraved themselves, bathing in their own indulgence for twenty long years. It sickened him to see what they had done to his mother and the million other folk across the Empire like her.

Marton had smiled as he killed his master. *I brought judgement down upon them, Mother. Something is better than nothing. They never broke my mind. Never.* His ears were still throbbing, and his eyes were twitching. He winced in pain as he scratched them. A vicious hum droned in his mind in place of what used to be the sounds of the world. But a thrill was still flowing through him from the Word—from the kill. He knew he should head straight for the tunnels. Mose would wait, and Marton could earn a favour by being there early. But as hard as he tried, Marton knew he couldn't leave his mother to die in all of this. She walked through a blazing fire to save his life once, he could walk beneath a falling star to save hers. She would never understand the Kiss of Silence, and she may not forgive him for the murder he'd committed, but he would at least save her life. He could drag her down to the tunnels with him. If he could do one thing for her in his petty, hopeless life, he could die happy.

He trekked through the golden streets and watched the raucous chaos revel out around him. It was a twisted menagerie of perversions. The Yehvenki had little hope and traded what they had left for carnal pleasures and violence. People hung from buildings, naked. Disembodied corpses littered the streets. Houses burned, wagons burned, people burned on stakes, and the smoke filled the narrow streets like a sauna. Marton covered his mouth with his arm and ignored the sights. *These folks will never know what it truly means to live. To take back their lives like I have.*

His mother's house was far enough away from the other fires that they hadn't damaged the small, one floor house. When the empire had taken Marton to serve the guard, they rewarded his family with a home. *They took my balls and gave my mother and sister a house. A real step up from our thatch and log house that turned into a pyre for dad. They didn't even charge Mom for the wayn that carried my sister's dead body when she died of black lung. And I was happy for it... happy for Mom to have such a peaceful life while I suffered.* Marton felt sick as he remembered the flames, his mother scooping him up like a bag of grain, her chest heaving against his cheek as she choked on smoke. His sister's cries, his father's screams, flaming bull banners, and the Warlock beneath that took them in. *"Your mom and sister could have this house, boy. All of it. Just give me your life and it is done."*

He knocked on the front door and tried to open it.

Someone had locked it.

"Mah?" he said. "It's me." There was still no answer. He looked in the window but couldn't see anything. He looked up. The star was taking up a third of the entire sky. It was black and burning and monstrous, like a demon descending from the heavens to kill the world. "Mom?" he yelled again. Finally, he busted the door down with his boot. The Word of power in his armour made it an effortless task.

Marton threw up when he saw his mom dead on the ground. She had taken a hammer to her own head. One clean blow to the centre of the forehead. Her cold hand was still clasping the hammer. Marton knelt down and let everything out of him. All the years of heartache and pain. The resentment and the suppressed adolescence. It all poured out of him. And his ears burned worse than ever. He felt like giving up. *But Mose will wait...* He couldn't give up, not now. Not after all of this. He could die with purpose. He needed to find meaning in his meaningless life. *I'm sorry, Mom. I'm so sorry I didn't come sooner.* But Marton knew that he was lying to himself. He rarely came to see her, not as much as a son should, and it tore at him every day. Even now, he only came so *he* could feel better. *You're a coward, Marton. You always have been. You can change that, if only for an hour, you can change.*

Marton closed his mother's eyelids and crossed her arms on her chest. He plucked a twig of lavender and a blooming marigold from his mother's garden and placed them on top of her hands.

"Rest easy, Mah. I'm sorry." Marton wiped a tear, then quickly forced himself out and back into the streets before he completely broke down weeping. *She might have been a Gramma in a different world. She would have been such a sweet Gramma.* Then he forced himself to run. *Mose will wait. He will wait. He is the only person who has ever loved you. He won't leave you. He won't...*

The gate to the tunnels was a spectacle amongst a spectacular city. It was a short, rounded tower, crowned with golden spires. A grand whiteoak door carved with green runes opened like a gaping mouth in the stone. The flaming bull banners of Yehven hung from each shoulder. Sorcerers had carved runes of holding and runes of concealment to look like intricate patterns woven together in a tapestry of hollowed stone lines. Without the charms in Marton's breastplate, he wouldn't see the door at all. To most, the tower looked just like the other obelisks erected throughout the Golden City. The Emperor had hoped the Abori wouldn't be able to find it if they hid it in plain sight. *I guess we'll finally find out.* There were dozens of the other guards standing around, looking frustrated. One saw Marton coming and shook his head.

"Mose isn't here." Marton could see the man's lips moving. Mose pointed at his ears, to the Kiss. The man scratched *his* ears. "He must not have made it," he mouthed. Marton put a hand to his forehead. His skull was throbbing.

I don't believe it. Mose wouldn't leave us... he wouldn't leave me...

"The master's chamber," Marton said. His tongue felt sloppy in his mouth, and he could only hear the humming of acid charred eardrums.

The guard's eye twitched. Another guard ran to Marton desperately. He was crying as he gripped Marton's head in between bony hands.

"The Abori have breached the walls." The man made sure Mose could see his lips as he squeezed his head tighter. "It's over. Mose has failed us."

Marton pushed the guard away. *Mose wouldn't fail—couldn't. Mose is everything I am not. Mose is perfect.* There was nowhere to run. The Abori would murder them all if they couldn't breach the whiteoak door. Each of them had the blood of masters on their souls now. Karaat would not judge them kindly.

He can't have failed us. He was so sure. I believed in him. Why did you believe in anything? Believe, believe, believe. Can't you?

Guards were banging the butts of their spears on the door, hopelessly; desperately. But there was no reply from the other side. Mose had not made it. The rebellion was over, just like that. The Golden City of Ailar was entirely under the shadow of the falling star, and the folk had succumbed to the darkness. Many of them were splatting down in the road, falling from high building tops. One of the Golden Guards standing by stripped his armour off and ran into the chaos, naked and chanting. Marton couldn't believe it was real. That it was really over. This was the end.

Mose... Mose will save us. He will be here. He will open the door, like he promised. Believe he will. Hold on to hope. Don't break. But deep down, Marton knew Mose hadn't failed. Deep down, he knew Mose had deceived him. Just as the empire had all those years ago. His runes of cunning had warned him all along, but he so desperately wanted to believe in something that he ignored the pangs of warning that the magics pulsed through his veins. Marton clenched his fists around his spear.

You know what happened. There is another door. You know there is another door because you have wandered there and touched the comet carved into the black stone door. Mose knows, too, he must. He is twice as cunning as you, even with your runes...

Marton hadn't even realized his legs had started moving. Something inside of him had awoken. His golden chestplate rattled, and his ears hummed as he ran. Through the throngs of drunken and desperate city folk. Through the pens of disturbed animals and their strained whines of distress. Into back alleys that smelled of piss and shit and animal feed, littered with stray corpses that lay blue and dead and covered in their own vomit. And there it was, radiant in the dim starlight. The black rune door. Marton stood completely still as if his legs had stiffened dead. He heard bare feet slapping on gold paved roads. And suddenly, Mose appeared from around the street corner. Marton stood beside a fishmonger's stall, still alight with the odour of its dealings, and watched the man approach the black stone door.

Mose? It looked almost like him, but he had changed enough that Marton couldn't be sure. The man who could be Mose wore a purple cloak covered in blood. He was alone. Marton watched as the man lingered a long moment before fumbling in his pockets to produce a keystone. *Go with him. If you were any kind of hero, you would show yourself and demand to go with him.* Marton winced as he scratched at his ears. The heavy stone door slid open. *Step out now, show yourself, and show Karaat you're not a coward. Prove it to yourself. Demand to go with him.* Marton watched as the man disappeared, the heavy door shutting tight behind him, and he didn't move.

The streets were empty, the stalls barren. The city of no sleep had finally begun to slumber. *Not a master anywhere. They're hiding, cowering underground like insects. That is no way to live.* Marton smiled. He was nothing but a coward. There was no place for him in the New World. He was ready to die. His joy came from knowing Mose would kill as many of the masters as he could. And his joy came from knowing that for one small moment, he had control of his life and made a choice.

Marton's smile faded as sorcerous lights erupted from the inner city. Shadows flickered through the narrow streets like a shaman's show. The Abori had breached the inner walls. There was nothing between the dream eaters and the guards now. Nothing between them and the tunnels but a small door.

Marton ran back through the alleyway and towards his fellow guards once more. When he arrived, there were far fewer of them standing than when he had left. The streets vibrated from thousands of bone clad feet marching in unison. The overwhelming presence of death had shrouded Marton like a wet blanket.

Don't be afraid. Marton couldn't stand up to Warlocks or Abori, but he could at least face death without fear. He could rise above his station for one last minute. But when he saw the Abori marching towards him, there was no fighting the terror rolling through him then. It rippled through his bones and paralyzed him to the spot. Row upon row of bone armoured warriors on dead horses trotted through the golden streets.

The Abori slaughtered every person they saw, swinging their wicked red swords from bone-faced horses as they rolled through the city like a calm wave of murder. In the middle of it all, on a raised platform carried by warriors with coloured inks carved in their bodies, was a woman in elaborate garbs. She had pink flowers woven in her yellow hair and wore a fine silk dress of all white. *She's beautiful...* She stood barefoot with her hands in the sky. Her eyes were closed and her mouth hung open in ecstacy, like she was at the very pinnacle of joy, singing to the sky. The way the other folk stared at her made Marton wish he could take back his Kiss, so he could hear one last thing of beauty before he died. Whatever she was singing must have been something elaborate. *She's calling the star down...* Marton watched the faces of his fellow guards light up with elation at the sight of her. "*Magi*" was on their lips. "*Mage...*"

Marton found that his jaw was open, and he struggled to look away. But as the Abori got closer, he watched them instead. He could see that each of them were Kissed by Silence as well. *They will see you as a brother.* Marton hoped. *A son.*

The Abori had come to watch the end of the Empire of Yehven and stomp out any cockroaches who dared live through the Starfall. It was just like the dreams the masters had. Marton had heard accounts of the dream eaters' nightmares his whole life. He smiled, thinking of death. He had served the empire for too long; done things he could never take back, and he had nothing for it. Even his mother, the only person who has ever loved him, left him in this world alone. He was ready for death.

The other Abori warriors garbed themselves in layers of black metals Marton had never seen before. They shimmered in the shadow of the Starfall, like gemstones. The Abori swarmed up main streets and crept out of dark alleyways, all wearing long hair in braids, dyed in bright hues of green and blue and pink. Many of them had tattoos etched into their skin with coloured inks. Some guards readied their weapons, but Marton dropped his spear. These folks were beautiful in the same way the Starfall was. They were pure—like Nature. They were clean. They were fighting for something bigger than themselves, and it was alive in the air around them—it pressed on his chest and made his heart work harder for each beat. Marton could never have imagined a sweeter death than one delivered by the Abori. They sloshed through pools of blood in the golden streets, and Marton fell to his knees and watched the bone-faced horses trot up on him with blood crusted hooves. He realized he was crying now, too.

One of the Abori dismounted. When Marton smiled at her, she smiled back. A sweet smile that touched his soul. Marton felt understood, and to feel understood was the most powerful feeling he'd ever had, stronger than the magics dancing on his tongue. The Abori woman kissed his forehead and held out a pair of manacles glowing a faint orange. Marton took them and strapped them around his wrists. No one had ever given him a choice before, and he wasn't used to it. If he had any choice at all, he would still have his testicles. Maybe he'd be married, or something. The thought seemed stupid.

But he used to see the master's children running around. Sometimes they would make him laugh, and he would wonder what it'd be like to have his own one day. Imagining it filled him with the feeling he had when he first gave his mom and sister their home—a feeling like he'd done something, and it was more than he'd felt in his whole life.

"Thank you," he muttered. His heart was bleeding pain, but when the Abori woman's wet lips touched his forehead again, he had never felt happier and never safer than in those chains. "Thank you..."

"Wait until I'm done with you, Marton, and see if you still want to thank me." The woman mouthed the words slowly. Marton smiled in awe. The woman moved on to the next guard and Marton knelt on the ground in her wake. *She knew your name...* he was so joyous he didn't even wonder how. *She knew your name...*

Ten Minutes to Starfall

THE ABORI SOBBED WHILE performing their work of butchery. But they didn't look upset. These were tears of joy. Of elation. This was the Starfall. The dream eaters had conjured this in nightmares for centuries. *This is a damn celebration for these people.* The black, screaming mass that was the star and a tiny little dot that must have been the sun were the only things in the burning red sky now. It was oddly beautiful. *Many people have died a less spectacular death.*

Marton knew his turn below the Abori's blade was coming. He was chained and splayed as the day the Warlocks cut his unborn children from between his legs, and the itch in his ears was driving him mad.

The woman who had chained him called herself Na'reen. She had moved her lips slowly to make sure Marton knew her name. She stood close enough to Marton now that he could see her skinny steel knife carved with glowing green runes. It looked to have come from another world.

Marton watched one of his Golden brothers squirm beside him as Na'reen leaned into him with the knife. *It's Benji. My god, Benji, why? You're too young for this. Too young.* Benji's face was red and twisted with horror as Na'reen did her work. With a neat precision, Na'reen cut off the thin strips of flesh that covered Benji's eyes. The eyelids peeled off easily once they were slit. *Like peeling a grape...* Benji hardly moved, the chains helped with that. When Na'reen finished cutting off his eyelids, she angled the wooden board so that he could only look straight up at the sky. *At the star...* Na'reen flicked the thin, wet skin of his eyelids away, and it stuck to the ground like fleshy phlegm. Then she knelt down and kissed Benji on the forehead. She looked up at Marton and smiled, her bright eyes glistening with tears. *You're next...* He felt that warmth in his stomach again. *Most folk die a much less spectacular death.* He kept telling himself that, and he believed it, too. *Mose. What are you doing, Mose? What is happening down there?*

Na'reen held the knife up to him. And then she was inside of his head.

"The Kiss... how cute... I don't need a voice to make you hear me. I want you to know why I'm cutting your eyes open. I want you to watch the Starfall. Every second. I want you to see death come down on you."

One, two, three, and it was done. The knife was so sharp, Marton didn't feel it until it was over. Both of his eyelids were gone. He couldn't believe how easily they were removed; the sense of duty with which she performed it. There was no resistance to the skin. He was crying now, too. Maybe from the beauty of the sky that had turned crimson and charcoal behind the falling star—but probably from the pain. *They pulled a flaming rock from the sky... it was them...*

"You hear me, Marton? Of the Abori, we are the Watchers. Through the lands, we slithered for years like snakes to find Her. Mage. Nature's child. The Old One has taught her the song of sky fall, and now the time has come for the Watchers to watch it happen. The Words die here, today. Nature wins, always."

They pulled a flaming rock from the sky... it was them... her...

All around Marton, the Abori were crying as they corralled and butchered all of the guards who weren't chained to boards. Marton could feel their power rolling inside himself—like their justice was contagious. Like the Abori were alive in *him. They will live forever... they are of the Earth.* Many hundreds, maybe even thousands of Abori had snaked their way down into the tunnels, with blue lips curled into smiles and tears carving rivers down their cheeks.

"But why? Why are you happy about this?" Marton asked. He wasn't sure if he'd asked aloud or only thought about it. But the Abori warrior heard him anyway and grinned.

"Because your people's souls are so lost to darkness, so corrupt and bleeding from these songs of eldritch madness, that freeing the tortured

things inside of you is the most beautiful thing our people could ever imagine—to free a bleeding soul. A beauty so great that our own souls flow out through our tears, and we will rest easy when our death soon follows. The Old One only gave this gift to the Honoured Ones of our people. Only we are given the opportunity to watch the sky fall while the rest of our people hide away in the wrinkles of time. It's a gift we have not taken for granted."

Na'reen tilted Marton's board back and strapped his neck in place with a belt. He could smell the freshly tanned leather. He could only see the star. The star was all there was.

"The song of the Empire has become too loud. Too consuming. Karaat and His Creator Gods have stretched their greedy hands too far into this world, and it's time to remove them and their creations. The war between the Natural Earth and the Creator Gods has gone on too long. Today, it ends. And you will watch it happen. Nature finds a way, always."

Marton was in so much pain that all he could do was laugh. He was twitching. *Mose. Mose you left us. You left us. Mose. Mother. I tried to stand up to them. I tried Mother. I'm a coward, Mother.* The heat from the star was intense now. He could feel his flesh burning. Blistering.

"Ten. Nine." The Mage was convulsing with euphoric passion as Na'reen counted.

The ground was shaking, and the pure energy from above was crushing him. *Are they counting down?* He thought he was screaming, but couldn't be sure. It felt so good to scream. *Oh, Mother, if you could only see how beautiful a comet is up close.* The comet billowed through the black-red sky, a shimmering mass. There was no doubt he was screaming now.

"Six. Five."

A rippling crash shook the ground as the comet broke through Earth's barrier. The clouds parted, as if the ocean in the wake of Karaat rising, and the star leaked into the sky like blackened blood.

Something in his throat tore from the screaming. The Abori were chanting the countdown. The woman on the raised platform was in some kind of arcane ecstasy. His flesh was melting off of his bones. *They never broke my mind, Mother. Never. The star is so beautiful. It's so–* A wicked pressure in his forehead felt like it might burst his skull. His eyes stopped working. His body was shaking. The earth shook violently beneath him. The pressure from above was crushing. *Mose... why?*

"Two. One."

There was only hot darkness.

THE BEGINNING

One Hour to Starfall

"This way, hurry." Mose held his hand out to lead Adeqor and Sera through the dark hallway.

"Something has happened here, Nine. The guards have rebelled against the masters. It's—ugh." Adeqor shuddered. He seemed to lose strength. *The harrisene will kick in about now. It has to. It will... careful, careful...* Mose could sense Adeqor's nervousness. Adeqor was not a dumb man. He would suspect Mose now, after learning of the rebellion, and Mose knew it.

"I had a feeling something was wrong. That's why I came back through these passageways. I wanted to make sure you were okay, master. You and Sera have been nothing but good to me all these years," he lied. "You could have left me to the wolves like our mother left my father, but you took in me and Cleo after he died." *As slaves and test subjects, and as the dying wish of our mother, I'm a bloody number to you... a number...*

Adeqor puffed out a deep breath.

"Well, I'm glad to hear you say that, Nine. Ahem." Adeqor coughed into his hand.

"Is that blood?" Mose asked. Adeqor wiped his bloody hand on his pant leg.

"We should—" Adeqor broke out into a more severe cough. He put a hand out and leaned against the wall. Mose grabbed one arm to keep him from falling. "I feel drowsy," Adeqor said, and looked at Mose like he was trying to decide whether to kill him or ask for help.

The Warlock sang a Word, and the dark hallways lit up with the warm glow of fire spirits. Adeqor could kill Mose in a second with a simple flapping of his tongue, and Mose knew it. He couldn't make a single mistake now. *Careful... don't slip. Careful...*

They came to a steep staircase leading into the streets of Ailar. Mose turned around to help Sera down the first step. Mose felt bad when Sera smiled heartily at him. She had always been so kind to him. It was Sera who insisted on keeping him around, that he looked just like family. *Because I am family...* She looked at Adeqor sternly. Adeqor cleared his throat again.

"Nine, I have always wanted to tell you I'm sorry," Adeqor said. Mose felt his stomach twist.

"Sorry?"

"For your sister. For everything. We are brothers. It doesn't matter that your father was a barbarian heathen. That was my mother's fault for taking him to bed. You are my blood. None of this is right," Adeqor said. He looked ashamed of himself. *Sorry? She didn't just take him to bed. They were in love. Love! My father talked of Mother every morning, day, night. Always. She had to hide their love from people like* you. *No, no you bastard, you don't get to be sorry. Sorry doesn't change a goddamn thing.* He could still hear his sister's chains chipping the marble floor when Adeqor dragged her away. *Sorry? No. I can't accept that. That is not enough.*

"Just ask him," Sera blurted. "I've had enough of this. The bloody sky is falling and still your hubris stands in the way." Sera threw her hands out to the side and started to sob. "Ask him! I'm sick of it!"

Adeqor scratched the back of his head. Mose spotted his identity stone hanging around his neck glinting ice-blue in the firelight. An apple-sized orb that the empire crafted with the old science for each Warlock upon birth. Identity stones were a symbol of the Warlocks' superiority over other earthly creatures. And that stone contained the magics that would get Mose access to the tunnels. It was his only key. *Sorry? This bastard says he's sorry? What does that change? Does sorry bring Cleo back? Does sorry bring back Dad? Sorry does nothing. Sorry changes nothing.*

Adeqor cleared his throat again. Whatever the Warlock had to ask must have been important to him. Mose could only think about what was important to *him*—vengeance for his sister and father.

"You see, Nine..." Adeqor started, but Sera fell into a sitting position like dead weight, and Adeqor rushed to her.

"I'm feeling a little flushed," she whispered. Adeqor rubbed her back. Mose could see that he, too, was fading. Sweating profusely and rubbing at his eyes like he thought that might calm the pain he must have felt there. Mose smiled. The harrisene would soon take over their limbs and paralyze them. Only moments from then, it would freeze their heart. Mose had control. At that moment, he owned Adeqor's life. *This... this is what you waited for. This is what power feels like. To hold a life in your hand like a soft fruit. To know the binding of one fist would destroy it entirely.*

"Sera!" Adeqor choked out a scream. He was shaking her unconscious body. "Sera, please don't leave me." Mose stood over him. He unsheathed his knife. Adeqor didn't even notice. That, and his hubris wouldn't allow him to. Adeqor looked up. "Would you come with us, Mose?" Adeqor blurted. Mose stared into Adeqor's eyes, glistening with welled tears. He saw love there. He saw a brother's care—acceptance. All too late. "Please, I need you to help me carry her. It would mean so much to her... to us... if you came."

"Come where?" Mose asked. And at that moment, Adeqor saw the knife. His face twisted into a scowl, and hateful realization replaced the love in his eyes. There was no time for contemplation, only immediate reaction. If Adeqor wanted to kill Mose, it would only take a single Word.

Mose stabbed his knife into Adeqor's right ear just as the Warlock formed a Word with his mouth. Once, twice, three times, four. It squelched in and out, and Mose's hand was sticky wet with blood. Mose let Adeqor's corpse fall to the ground with a fleshy smack. He turned around and held his fingers to Sera's neck. She was already cold.

When he was sure they were both dead, Mose got to work. He took Adeqor's robe off before blood could soak it more than it already had. Then he took both of their identity stones. A perverse smile twisted on to his face as an unexplained energy surged through his blood. He felt *awake*. More so than he ever had. And the aches and pains in his arms and back had faded to nothing. *This is the power of a soul bound with the Words. Folk will bow down to you. You are the New Order...* Then he donned the purple cloak, the shoulders still soaked with Adeqor's warm blood.

He tucked Sera's stone away in the deep purple pocket and held the other in his left hand. Then he picked up the book. The true prize. Insa Rolin's notebook. Mose had heard Adeqor tell Sera the value of that book countless times. Insa had learned the secrets of the world from studying the Old Ones. There were pages in that book that could give Mose the power of the Creator Gods. He flipped through the pages. *Where, where, where?* He couldn't take the whole book without raising suspicion. He couldn't risk anyone but himself having it. His fingers were bloody as he tore through page after page. *Where!*

"Where!" Mose could feel the power of the stone, the power of the comet, and he was shaking when his eyes finally saw what they had been seeking. *The Word that kills aging. The Necro.* Mose tore the page carefully from the rough binding. He neatly folded it and tucked it into the purple robe.

Mose plucked a wall sconce and lit Insa Rolin's life's work on fire. Not even the darkest magics conjured in the darkest recesses of the darkest minds could live up to fire in her majesty. The flame rolled on as the sun and the moon. Even after the Starfall, fire will roll, forever.

Mose watched the book shrivel into blackened ash. And with a confidence he'd never felt before, he drifted like smoke towards the tunnels. If the masters caught him, he was ready to kill every one of the New Order. *If they won't bow breathing, they will lay before you breathless.*

Every noble aristocrat of the Yehvenki Empire had gathered in one place to hide from the Starfall. They had been arriving in caravans for months from all corners of Edura, each more grand than the last. The New Order didn't even try to hide what they were doing from the smallfolk. *But they should have hid from you, yes.* Something about having more power than a falling star made Mose giddy. There was a swagger to his step like he'd never had.

Mose emerged from the innards of the glass towers down a staircase that led to a back alleyway. He was somewhere in the middle of the tower district, right in front of the entrance to the tunnels. This entrance was not the same door he had told the rebellion to meet at. The slaves and Golden Guards of the rebellion would gather at a similar door, not far away, that led to nothing. When Mose needed them, they would be close. For now, he had to be alone. *Why are you afraid? After all of this, you are going to let fear invade your thoughts?*

He walked up to the blackstone door. He had an odd feeling that someone was watching him. He looked around and saw only the abandoned stalls of mongers. The blackstone door was unlike anything else in Ailar. It was a stark contrast to the gold paved streets and whitewashed towers and glass domes. Runes of holding were carved into the door to make it impenetrable, and runes of concealment kept it hidden. Without Adeqor's identity collar and the magics that were now running through his body, Mose wouldn't even be able to see this door. *It's here... it's really here.* The stone was cool on his calloused hand, and he ran his finger along the carved lines of the runes. The symbol of a comet was etched deep into the centre.

He took a deep breath and unfolded the page he tore from Insa's book. With a Word, he could kill even the most powerful Warlocks on earth. Insa Rolin had transcended humanity. He'd turned himself into a living god. Able to bring forth or banish anything he pleased. The Empire should have killed him long ago. He should never have been able to gain the knowledge he did. He should never have been able to do what he did to living things. When Cleo came back from Insa's dungeons, she wasn't Human anymore. He had turned her into a twisted Creation. He had heard Adeqor say countless times that the empire should have never allowed his book to exist. That if it got into the wrong hands... Adeqor never seemed to finish that sentence.

Their deaths are their own doing. You are merely the harbinger of the New World Order.

Mose had it all under control now. He would use Adeqor's keystone to open the door and mutter the Word of stillness. Once the Warlocks couldn't move, he would strap them down to a table, one by one, just like they did to his sister. He would torture them for as long as it pleased him. There would be decades of darkness after the Starfall. With Words of obedience, he could keep his rebellion quelled. Let them simmer until he needed them to boil over again. *When the sun pierces the darkness again, you will be God. When the skies are born again, you will be reborn with them.* Mose folded the page and tucked it deep into Adeqor's purple robe. Then he touched Adeqor's identity stone to the comet. The runes lit up with a brilliant glowing gold, and the door swung open, heavy and harsh, grinding Mose's ears.

Mose walked in. The Word of stillness on the tip of his lips. *Would it even work on this lot? What if they have charms in the tunnels to prevent such things?* Suddenly, he wasn't as confident in his plan. He followed the tunnels down and down deeper. *Where are they? Why was no one guarding the entrance? Are they that sure of themselves? No, you're at the wrong place. Of course. This leads to nothing. You've been fooled.* But he carried on.

Flames danced in rusted sconces along the cave walls, and cold water dripped from the ceiling as Mose descended further and further into the crust of the earth. *There is no time for this to work. It would take the guards too long to descend. Too long. Turn back.* But Mose couldn't stop himself from moving down and down, and down. Finally, Mose came to a white stone door carved with green, glowing runes. His identity stone lit up as he neared, and when he touched the stone to the door, it swung open.

Hundreds of folks in purple robes all stared at him in the gaping maw of the door. Mose felt the Word creep onto his tongue. He opened his mouth...

"Adeqor? Is that you?"

...and then closed it again. One Warlock was walking towards him with narrowed eyes. He was trying to recognize him. *Adeqor had hidden away so long these people have forgotten what he looked like.* Mose whimpered. He had to sell that he'd been through something drastic to explain the blood.

"It's me." He fell to his knees. The man ran to his side.

"Where is Sera?" The man put his hand on Mose's back. "What happened? We didn't think you would come." Mose looked up at him, stared into his eyes. *Kill him. This is what you've been waiting for.* But Mose saw something in those eyes he hadn't seen before. This was Bazal, the great and powerful, and he was looking at Mose like an equal. "It's me," Bazal said. "I know it's been a while. I should have checked on you sooner up in your tower. Where is Sera? Are you okay?"

Mose could feel the warmth in Bazal's voice heating his icy heart. No one had ever spoken to him as an equal. No one had ever cared about him. Even though it was false, it felt better than anything he'd ever known. He let the Word of stillness slip down his tongue and swallowed it. He let himself fall into the open hole of his heart. As he dug himself further into all of the pain, he broke down sobbing. He fell to the ground like a sack of grain. That's when a horrible thought struck him. *Yora and Ren. Surely they would recognize you.* Mose scanned the room. Everyone was staring at him. His heart thumped so loud he was sure Bazal could hear it.

"It's okay now, Adee, you're safe here." Bazal picked him up under his arms and embraced him. Mose choked out a few words between whimpers.

"My own guards killed her... I would have–" He tried to cover his face. *If Yora was here she would have reacted. Sera was her closest friend.*

"It's okay. You're with us now," Bazal said. And Mose felt that great hole gape wider, and tears poured out of it. He wasn't sure why. Maybe he felt relieved. He had an out. Maybe he didn't want revenge, just to be cared for. To belong. The conflict didn't bother him. It only meant that it wasn't all over. That this wasn't the end. Not for him.

The massive entrance hall went on and on, with corridors stretching in all directions like roots. Mose looked around at the faces he saw. These weren't the rulers of the Yehvenki Empire, these were the working class elite. Ellorin and her Banshee; Bazal and his hundred masters; the soothsayers. This was not the same group of nobles who had been gathering from all parts of the Empire on grand caravans. These were not the empresses and emperors and their retinues. There weren't nearly enough of them. It seemed those nobles had simply vanished. This was something else. *It was this lot that killed the Emperor, and only Karaat knows how many others. This was a rebellion that had succeeded without ever making a single sound. One class exterminated another. This is something worth living for.* A cult of death. The Creators could respect someone who rose amongst this lot. This was where Mose belonged. Not mucking around with the slaves and guards. Mose always knew he was capable of more. That his destiny led to something greater. With what he had left of Insa's book, he could change the world. He could help mold the New World into something beautiful. *You could live forever...*

"We made our deal with the gods. Karaat and the Creators have kept us alive." A man with a long grey beard and long grey hair to match crept forward from the shadows. *Eralis. Had he taken Creon's place as emperor after their cult had murdered him?* His voice echoed through the chambers. "We paid the price of sacrifice and let the Old One take the victim's soul. We fed the inner earth with the soul of an emperor. Only the Ailaryan Order remains now, and the Abori will not find us here. We have Karaat's protection. Karaat has told it true. We will live to see the sun again. This will be a long many years, but if we work together, we can create a New World. One where the Ailaryan Order are gods." A soft cheer erupted, including Mose. *But you're not Mose anymore, no. The Order had enslaved Mose. Adeqor is a master's name. And that is what you've become—a master.*

"So, you're wondering, what is our end of the deal?" Eralis said. Mutters amongst the crowd bid him continue. "The Great God Karaat gains power through worship and sacrifice. The fewer people who believe in him, the less powerful his Words are. Karaat has taken most of the minds on earth by this point. His power is undeniable. The Words are supremely powerful and we, non-supreme beings, have lost control of our own minds. The Words have infected us, to where it is questionable if many of our leaders were actually in charge of their own actions. The Abori and the Starfall will wipe out most of the believers. Karaat's power will fade enough so that the Words will lose their power. And when the world awakes from its long slumber, and the survivors are crawling about in muck and filth, struggling to live day to day, we will be there. We will bring our knowledge and our understanding of the land, its seasons, and the cycles of the stars. And the Words, however faint their powers are, will appear as sorcery. We will keep the memory of Karaat's song alive. We will ensure his worship never fades. And in exchange, we will be gods on earth. The Ailaryan Order will rule everything." Eralis raised his fist to the air. With his other hand, he banged on the flag hanging from the lectern in front of him. It was a black flag with the symbol of a comet in orange. The symbol of the Ailaryan Order. Mose had seen the comet carved into worn old stone but seeing it now—seeing it alive—made him wonder about the power it might hold and all the wonders that it might bring. *The god of gods uses such symbols—the sun, the moon—to garner worship.*

"Now that the comet in the sky is as real as the stars, it demands divinity." Eralis held the flag high above his head. The small crowd of Warlocks erupted into a cheer that Mose would have previously not thought possible from their kind. They usually leaked emotion as rocks bled, but now it poured out of them like Eralis had opened a wound. Mose couldn't help but join in. It felt so good to let it out.

"The Ailaryan Order!" they all belted out in an eerie, cult-like unison. *Nothing like folks coming together,* Mose thought and laughed to himself. *The guards will think the door I sent them to was false. They will think I have deceived them.* He wanted so badly to feel sorry for them. He wanted so badly to feel bad about himself. *This wasn't the plan. No. It's better than your plan. Be honest with yourself. It was never really going to work. You were always going to die trying to fight these people. You just had to mask it with this rebellion because you're too afraid to face it head on. You were too afraid to face it and still are.* He wanted so badly to feel sorry for the guards and the enslaved. All the folk out there like him and Cleo, pulled away from their families and made to serve another. But he couldn't. Mose only felt joy. Pure, unrivalled joy at the thought of a new life.

Suddenly there was banging on the door. Louder and louder, and the screams from the other side were worse than the banshee's. *The Abori.* The walls were shaking from their fury. And the door held. The Abori's screams became louder and louder as if they were filling the narrow hallway outside. Mose could feel the terror seeping out of the Warlocks, seeping out of himself. *If they break this door, we are all dead.* Mose had feared the Abori all his life. He had feared *them* more than death. Maybe that was why he was willing to risk so much to get into these tunnels. The white door cracked. The Abori's cries melting in through the cracks were more deafening than the falling star.

"They will not breach, Karaat has told it true." Eralis stepped down from his dais and stood in front of the white door. "They will not breach." His voice cracked and his hands were trembling. And as the crack in the door grew and the stone walls splintered at the hinges, Mose remembered his sister. *One day, we can be them, Mose.*

I know that one of us will live forever. One of us will be the Sun and the Moon, or more than that. One of us will be a god. We can make it true, Mose. In this world, anything you can dream is possible. Da told me that. He loved you so much.

The door shook, and the droning screeches of the Abori grew louder. Eralis held his hands to the ceiling. "The star is upon us. I feel it now." The old Warlock held his hand to his chest and collapsed like his legs had become boneless. Ellorin picked him up. "Brace for the impact, there is no way to know what this will feel like."

"Ten. Nine. Eight." Deep voices echoed in unison from somewhere in the tunnels. The soothsayers had awoken. Mose tried to see them in the dark, but the soothsayers wouldn't be seen in full. Only their yellow eyes glowed in the shadows and spoke a warning that said "look away."

Eralis began to hum Words of holding in a low note. "Come, everyone, hurry." The door cracked and splintered as the Abori pummeled it with eldritch magics, but the door was cursed with darker stuff from times of old and it held. Sorcerous winds and stenches crept in from the cracks. Fungus and moss came up from the ground below and tried to suck at Mose's feet. The other Warlocks all stood before the door and joined in with Eralis's song as they kicked away the earth magics that pulled at them from below.

"Adeqor. Come. Quickly," Bazal said. Mose nodded. Subconsciously, he touched the piece of paper that held Insa Rolin's darkest secrets. *The Necro.*

Mose hurried over and began to hum. *Adeqor. I have always liked that name. A true Warlock's name, that. Yes, that is who you will be. That will serve well, oh, yes.*

"Four, Three," the soothsayers sang in their ancient tongues, louder than even the Warlocks. And at that moment, the man who was once Mose knew that the Abori would not kill him on that day. The man who was once Mose would now be Adeqor, and Adeqor would live forever. *A god, Cleo, one of us will be a god. We will rise, and keep rising, Cleo. I promise.*

"Two, One."

And the entire world shook. The white door rattled violently but never broke. And it kept rattling as dust fell from the ceiling, and whatever twisted magics that held the cracked door and weakened hinges together had remained strong. The flames ceased to dance in their wall sconces and left the tunnels in cool darkness. The Sorcerers of old had built these tunnels to withstand anything—even time. The Abori were no longer screaming. Bazal looked at Adeqor and shrugged. A sly smile crept onto Adeqor's face. Slowly, he traced his chest to the pocket that held Insa Rolin's darkest songs. He fingered it softly and let his mind flood with wondrous possibilities. It was a wicked wonder that danced in Adeqor's mind as Eralis re-lit the wall sconces one by one, and the Warlocks hugged one another in relief. A gloriously wicked kind of wish—that his song would be the last ballad to ring out for all of eternity.

So it begins.

FROM THE AUTHOR PLEASE READ!

D EAR READER,

We did it! We're here, together, at the end. If you've read this far—Hi! I wholeheartedly hope you enjoyed *The Sound Of Starfall*. If you have indeed enjoyed your time here and you would like to support the series further, it would mean the world to me if you left an honest review on <u>Amazon</u> and <u>Goodreads.</u> Honest reviews help books reach a wider audience and give new authors like myself a chance to grow. You are the true heroes of this story, and your support is the lifeblood of this series.

Until the next Verse,
Scott Palmer

Join The Feldarra

Join The Last Ballad community! If you haven't already, sign up for my mailing list at scottpalmerauthor.com/mailinglist

And I would love to hear from you! Please, reach out. Let's chat about magic, and cats, or whatever...

Email : Scottpalmerauthor@gmail.com

Facebook: Scott Palmer

Insta:@scottpalmerauthor

X: @SPalmerauthor

Goodreads: Scott Palmer

Amazon: Scott Palmer

Glossary

Places and Events:

Edura - (eh-dur-ah) The Easternmost continent of the Known World. Known as *"the heart of existence."*

Yehven - (yeh-ven) Before it had expanded to a continent wide empire, Yehven was only a modest city located where The Raas River meets The Old Sea. After the Sorcerers disappeared, The Warlocks that ruled Yehven moved thousands of miles up river to the Golden City of Ailar and named their empire for the city of their birth.

Ailar - (ale-ar) The Golden City. A grand and luxurious city paved in gold and shaded by ivory statues, glass towers, and pyramids of solid gem. Built by the Sorcerers to withstand time itself and swollen with mystery.

Meylara - (may-lAR-ah) A slaver city. Slaves are bred and bought and sold here as a main export. Many strange magics are conjured in the dusty dark alleyways and crowded streets of Meylara, and people often travel here to find answers that have otherwise eluded them. The Meylarran people tend to have an aura of mystery to them as well, populated mostly by mongrels and inbreds of mixed ancient bloods; the Sorcerers have subjugated them out of fear and misunderstanding since the skies were new.

The tunnels - The name for the labyrinth of connected tunnels and underground palaces chiseled into the bedrock beneath Ailar and its surrounding mountains. The Warlocks believe the tunnels were carved out by the Sorcerers, but other theories have left the truth ambiguous.

The Starfall - The Abori's name for their ritual in which a mage of Nature pulls a star down from the sky to erase all below it.

CHARACTERS:

Adeqor - (a - deh - kor), A Warlock of Ailar, married to Sera. Once a high ranking user of magics famous for his work with Insa. Has been locked away in self imposed exile for twenty-seven years.

Sera - (s - AIR - ah), A Warlock of Ailar, married to Adeqor.

Yora - (yore - ah), A Warlock of Ailar, married to Ren.

Ren - A Warlock of Ailar, married to Yora.

Nine - (like the number 9), Servant to Adeqor.

Bazal - (bah - zil), A Warlock of Ailar. Leader of the Hundred Masters, and old friend of Adeqor and Sera.

Insa Rolin - (in - sah Roe - lin), A Warlock of Ailar. Famous for his adept use of magics. Considered a hermit and isn't bothered by the Empire as long as he doesn't bother them. Considered the most powerful wizard alive.

Dante - (DON - tay), A Warlock of Ailar.

Mose - (m - ohz), An enslaved man of Yehven. Brother to Cleo.

Cleo - (klEE - oh), An enslaved woman of Yehven. Sister to Mose.

Marton - (mar - tun), A Golden Guard in the service of Ailar. Brother to Lyanna.

Lyanna - (lee - ann - ah), An enslaved woman of Yehven. Sister to Marton.

Oliander - (oh - lee - and - err), A prophet of Karaat. Known for brainwashing folk and starting death cults within the ranks of Warlocks.

Myril - (meer - ill), An enslaved man of Yehven.

Creon - (cree - on), The Grand Emperor of Yehven and King of Ailar.

Na'reen - (nAH - reen), An Abori Warrior.

Benji - (ben - jee), A Golden Guard of Ailar.

Ellorin - (el - oh - rin), A Warlock of Yehven. The Queen of the Banshee.

Eralis - (eh-rAH-lis), The leader of the Ailaryan Order. A prophet of Karaat.

THE PEOPLES OF OLD:

Sorcerers - A race of Makers that served the Creator God Karaat. The Sorcerers vanished from the earth many centuries ago and are believed by the Warlocks to have become gods.

Warlocks - A race of magic users conjured up by the Sorcerers as a tribute to the Creator Gods.

Soothsayers - Nothing is known of the soothsayers other than that they know all things. The Soothsayers live in the shadows of the past and dream in the darkness of many tomorrows. Sometimes they speak.

Singers - A people who are bred and trained to live in the dark inner echo chambers of the gemstone pyramids and project their voices upwards to the clouds. Using magics, the Warlocks breed the Singers to be blind, deaf, and immobile with remarkably big chests and lungs as well as vocal coords that are as strong as steel. Warlocks extract the vocal cords of dead Singers and use them as unbreakable bow strings.

Draku - A race created by Insa Rolin and hidden away. Little is known about Draku other than their strange resistance to fire.

CULTS & GODS:

The Abori - A mysterious death cult from the wild lands of the north beyond the Shaded Arbor. They sing songs and conjure magics in the name of Nature and her children. It is prophesied that the Abori will bring the Starfall and invade the great Golden City of Ailar.

Dream eaters - A cult of Abori who have mastered the Old Ways and know how to visit others in their dreams. They work tirelessly, passing down their practice from generation to generation, to continue their slow assault on the minds of the Warlocks. Each night, the dream eaters send nightmares of an Abori invasion to the sleeping minds of Warlocks. Every night the dream eaters channel visions of extermination and of violence and as they are transmitting it with magics into the minds of their enemies, they are worn down with it themselves.

Yehvenki Empire - The flaming bull banners of the Yehvenki Empire fly over most of The Remembered Lands. Ruled by the race of Warlocks, Yehven has not known a threat in more than a millennia.

Aristocrats - The ruling class elite of the Warlocks. The classification is usually defined by bloodlines traced back to the very first Warlocks.

The New Order - The group of ruling class elite gathered by Grand Emperor Creon from all across Edura to hide from the starfall and live out the dark days in the tunnels.

The Ailaryan Order - A rebel order created by Eralis to overthrow the New Order and take the tunnels for themselves.

Creators - The Creators fell into the earth before the sky was born and only rarely surface.

Karaat - (kah-rat) The Creator God. Karaat gifts mortal beings with the gift of magics in exchange for undying respect and worship.

The Old One - A god of The Abori. The Old One birthed the ocean with a single tear and all of the land with a strand of hair.

WORDS:

Haruka - *Obedience*

Ventes - *Destroy*

Irill Tur Sa'Illes - *Speak true and enter*

WHAT'S NEXT?

Continue the story with the First Verse of The Last Ballad, A Memory of Song. Available where books are sold.